Kankakee County
Tales of Horror
Vol. 3

Kankakee County Tales of Horror

Vol. 3
The Awakening

From The Master Of Horror, Comes Book Three,
With Ten Spine Tingling Tales Of Horror,
To Scare The Life Back In Your Frightened Bones

Written by
Jesse Rodriguez

Copyright © 2009 by Jesse Rodriguez.

COVER ART, AND ILLUSTRATIONS BY JESSE RODRIGUEZ

SINISTER SAM CREATED BY SHIRLEY JONES-RODRIGUEZ

Library of Congress Control Number:	2009913189
ISBN: Hardcover	978-1-4500-1115-0
Softcover	978-1-4500-1114-3
EBook	978-1-4500-0264-6

All rights reserved. No part of this book may be reproduced or transmitted in any form or by any means, electronic or mechanical, including photocopying, recording, or by any information storage and retrieval system, without permission in writing from the copyright owner.

This is a work of fiction. Names, characters, places and incidents either are the product of the author's imagination or are used fictitiously, and any resemblance to any actual persons, living or dead, events, or locales is entirely coincidental.

These original stories were taken from the nightmares of scared souls, in the dead of night.

This book was printed in the United States of America.

To order additional copies of this book, contact:
Xlibris Corporation
1-888-795-4274
www.Xlibris.com
Orders@Xlibris.com

TABLE OF HORRORS

1. CITY OF THE DEAD 9
2. THE LAKE PRINT 25
3. GHOST HOUSE.. 34
4. ATTIC EYES 40
5. THE CREEPER 46
6. THE WEREWOLF OF BRADLEY........................... 54
7. DEMON PIT 62
8. FIREWOOD 70
9. THE BRADLEY CHUPACABRA............................ 78
10. CLAWS 88

CITY OF THE DEAD

I remember when it was called Kankakee, a noisy well-lit city with lots of excitement day, or night. Even the crime in the street was worth reading about in the local newspaper. Kankakee was a fishing community with plenty of parks, and shopping centers. Restaurants filled the city with too many to choose from when one was hungry for a bite to eat. Today that bite comes from a whole different way of life, for you see Kankakee is now called, THE CITY OF THE DEAD. A virus was discovered in a local animal hospital that soon consumed the city, causing the dead to come back to life. The living dead had taken over the city of Kankakee, and surrounding areas, or was it to be worldwide?

Here's how it all started, it was a calm day at the animal hospital; the local veterinarian was working on an anti-virus for distemper, when he discovered, by accident that what he was working on was about to shock the world in a catastrophic way. He was treating a dog for distemper that was dying on his operating table; Introducing Dr. Jones, he thought, what a perfect opportunity to try out his new anti-virus that he had been working on for many years.

CITY OF THE DEAD

At that very moment an injured dog was brought in, it was bleeding internally, apparently from a car accident. Dr. Jones placed the anti-virus on the exam table, then he went to get needed materials to treat the dog. The dog began to shake, and quiver causing the anti-virus on the exam table to fall over onto the injured animal. That's when it happened; at this point the dog had died. A mixture of this canine's dead blood must have mixed with the anti-virus, causing this chemical reaction of horror.

The doctor noticed the animal was dead, so he left him there on the exam floor; Dr. Jones went to attend to the other pets that were in need of medical attention. That instant the dog came back, to some sort of life, his eyes were fiery red, sharp fangs began to grow out of his mouth, and a stunning metamorphosis started to take place. The rabid canine began to attack everyone in sight.

The beast crashed through a window in the animal hospital and went on a killing rampage. The beast infected everyone in sight that it attacked. People that were bit were dying, and coming back to life as zombies. Soon the city was crawling with the living dead. It happened so fast that it was hard to control. Before anyone knew what had hit them, the city was overtaken, the living dead were everywhere. Chaos filled the city.

The police were out in the streets trying to control the violence that had spilled out, onto the city. The citizens were purchasing handguns at an alarming rate, out of fear for their lives no doubt. The living dead were too much for us to handle, for you see we had to eventually sleep, and that's when they took us out. Soon the zombies had taken over the east side of town. The police, and fire units set up perimeters to seal off this quadron of the city.

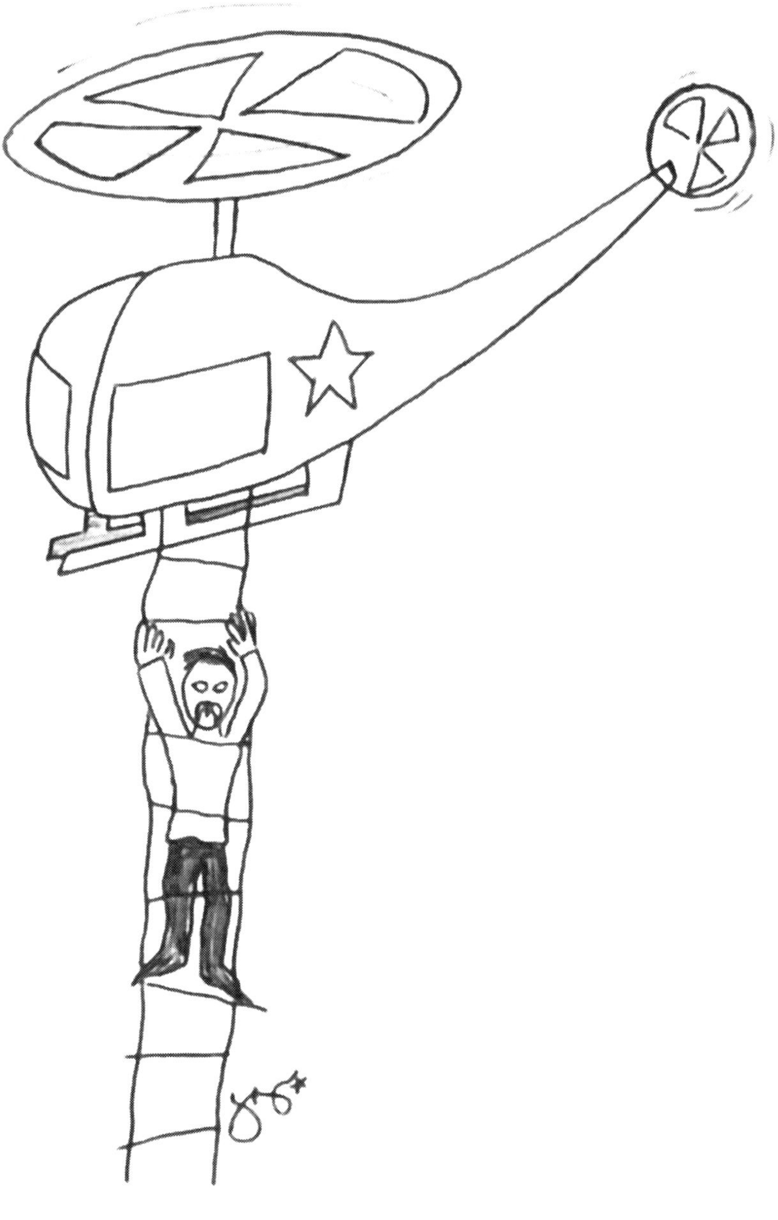

Nightfall came, and when it was too hard for us to see, the living dead attacked the perimeters in legions, and broke through. The dead were too powerful; their numbers were too great for the local police force of seventy officers. Many of the officers died in the devastation. The dead were moving into the downtown area, that night I saw the dead, feasting on the living, in the streets of Kankakee.

I saw automobiles crashing into each other, from the chaos in the streets. Gunshots rang throughout the city, like thunder. Fire and smoke were visible from a distance, Kankakee looked like a war zone. A number of zombies were seen working together, to push a transit bus on its side. The occupants never saw it coming; soon the zombies broke through the windshield, and began to feast on the fallen prey. Sounds of horror could be heard from the bus. The police did not even attempt to go near the bus, or help in any way. People could be seen jumping out of nearby buildings to escape the terror, only to fall to their death. The living dead had made their way into the buildings causing people, out of fright, to leap to their death. Fires were seen all over the downtown area, smoke filled the city.

A convoy of trucks filled with national guardsmen was out in numbers shooting the zombies. They had to be shot straight in the heart, for you see, that was the only way to take them down. A bullet, or sharp object through the heart, because nothing else affected them. You could burn them, or cut off a limb, and they still kept coming after you. The city was overtaken in a matter of days. The once populated city of Kankakee was now a calm desolate ghost town. The dead bodies of some of the zombies could be seen rotting in the streets like a bomb fell on the city.

Today a large concrete fence surrounds the city of the dead; Kankakee is a prison you might say, for these flesh-eating ghouls. The National Guardsman set up a perimeter in Bradley. To contain the virus, a team of scientist began to work day, and night studying the living dead. Soldiers patrolled the city of Bradley; a curfew was set up to protect the people. Martial law was in effect; anyone seen out after dark was to be shot, with the assumption he, or she might be one of the living dead.

Only special vehicles were allowed after dark, white vans, or white automobiles were used, with plenty of roadside checks. Although one could always sneak out at night in the cover of darkness, to take a peek at the dead. The army was not very alert. I had gone out at night a few times, by way of the cemetery path near Brookmont Boulevard. There was a set of tracks that led to Route 50, just a half a block from one of the retaining walls. The army guys slept through most of the guard time, allowing me to move about, in the cover of darkness.

Myself, and my brother Joe climbed a nearby tree, to take a gaze at the, CITY OF THE DEAD. The dead could be seen walking around looking for flesh, or blood should I say. The scent of death was in the air, and the zombies had a new home, Kankakee! They moved around pretty slow, I wondered if we could outrun them. Well tonight we were going to find out, armed with handguns, and stupidity we climbed over the retaining wall that surrounded the fortress of the living dead.

I wanted to see what had become of the courthouse located in the heart of Kankakee. We slipped through the army guardsmen under the cover of darkness to a nearby railway track that led to the train depot in the heart of the city. The walking dead were everywhere; they appeared to be walking in circles, or just looking for a place to go. Then we heard it! A helicopter landed on the roof of the courthouse. Soldiers rushed to open the doors. What were soldiers doing at the courthouse?

I had to get a closer look without the zombies noticing us. We did not want to attract attention by firing at them; we had to see what the soldiers were up to. Joe went to hotwire a vehicle for us to get as far away from the courthouse as possible, until we could figure something out. Joe pulled up slowly in a Dodge Charger, what a perfect car for speed if we had to elude the soldiers. We saw a white van at a distance, so we turned off the car and watched them move about at night. I saw what looked like the occupants of the truck were unloading bodies into the Kankakee River, but why? This is no way to contain a virus. If the virus made its way down the river other communities would be infected, our drinking water would be infected!

What was the army thinking? Then we saw it! The two guys unloading the bodies into the river were zombies themselves! Somehow they were evolving into something different, but how? The living dead could now drive, nor reason? We moved forward to get a closer look as they got back into the van, then we followed closely. The zombies were pulling into the police station. Several zombies were outside; it appeared as if they were communicating with each other. They were armed, and wearing soldier uniforms.

We watched as the zombies filled the back of the van, it was obvious that the takeover was through the river; the living dead had found a way out of the city. What we saw earlier were not bodies being disposed of at all, but the living dead, letting the river current take them to other locations via the river. We didn't even see it coming. Somehow we had to get the word out to the army in Bradley, before it is too late, or we had to stop them now, those were the choices.

Joe said he had an idea, he said "we should overtake a white van, get out of the city, and when they check us, tell them what we saw." No! I said, here's what we'll do, find a gas station, and burn the police station, and courthouse. That was the plan we made our way to the gas station on the corner of Station Street, and Washington Avenue. We filled several cans with gasoline, and now we were ready to create a diversion that would lure the living dead away from the courthouse.

We have to blow up the gas station, and then wait for them to react. Joe made a trail of gas from the gas station to the train depot. In few seconds we had to be ready to move at lightning speed. I saw Joe light the gas then a huge explosion rocked the city; we saw flames reach eighty feet in height, now that really got the ghouls attention. Zombies poured out of the courthouse like ants, and headed for the explosion, we could see their trucks, and other vehicles make their way to the explosion.

Joe rolled down the window, and started shooting at any zombies he saw. We drove over to the courthouse, and lit the place on fire. Then we drove over to the police station to do the same; soon the living dead would make their way back to us. These two places had to be wiped off the face of the city. The command centers they had set up were now up in smoke. The helicopter full of zombies, and the trucks full of zombies, were after us, we had to escape, and fast. I headed for the viaduct near the Kankakee Dam, to prevent from getting shot at, not that they could catch us in this Charger, but a helicopter can outrun any car.

Once in the viaduct we got out of the car, and made our way in the darkness to the nearby riverbank, climbing the retention walls was not an option. After eluding the zombies we approached a small motorboat by the riverbed, quickly we set off down the river towards the Bird Park area. We sped along the river, and then decided to cut the motor, and use the oars, to continue undetected in the deep of night. The living dead were everywhere, we could see them walking along the shore, but they dared not go into the raging river.

The zombies approached the shore and watched us row by; with their heads up high sniffing the air, it was as if they could smell us. The small boat drifted towards Bradley; soon we would have to make our way to the shore. We had to find a way back home, or to the soldier's camp. We had to warn the army, we had to let them know what was going on, in the CITY OF THE DEAD. Then we saw a disturbing site, zombie soldiers patrolling Bradley, it was too late. In the little time we were in the CITY OF THE DEAD, the zombies had taken over Bradley. It was time to move on.

We paddled out to the middle of the river, and coasted along undetected in the still of the night. We had to follow the river to the next town. We wondered, if our homes were victims of this plague. The zombies were taking over, how long before we were outnumbered was the question? We decided to pull over to the shore near some anchored boats; I had to switch boats with one that had more speed. We had to warn people, of the impending disaster that was about to hit the world. As we approached a landmass that was called the State Park, we waited to see if it was clear, then we hid the boat, and made our way along the highway. Using the cover of some nearby bushes, we waited to see who, or what might come down the highway.

Then there it was, an army convoy, but they were the living dead. After they drove by, I knew we had to stop them, but how? We needed grenades but we didn't have any, we had to distract the last vehicle, and take it undetected from the rest of the convoy.

The last truck was far enough; we rushed onto the truck by each side door, and then plunged a knife into the heart of the driver. He didn't even see it coming. The truck was ours, now all we had to do was slip away, by falling behind.

We drove the truck into the woods to see what it was loaded with. The truck was filled with medicine bottles, and syringes. What was it? The bottles were marked "DECEPTION" we knew hit the mother load; this must be what they were taking to help them cope with coordination. When the virus attacks the bloodstream all coordination, and motor skills are lost. The drug in the vials was the weapon they were using to cope with the transformation. This is why they could reason, and use weapons, drive vehicles, and plan our demise, but how did they get it?

The truck was also filled with cases of automatic weapons. This was it, in order to destroy the living dead, we had to find a way to poison the drug, and send the truck back to them. I drove to the nearby park ranger station, and we broke into the park office. Once inside we knew what to look for, drain opener, or rat poison. We worked all night tainting the bottles of their wonder drug. Soon they would feel the wrath of mankind again. Then we could take back our city, once they are weakened, we will hit them hard.

It was time, so we drove the truck back to the destination, from where we took the precious cargo. The guns, of course we had to keep. Once they notice all the weapons are missing, they will send troops of zombies after us, and they will take the drug back to their stronghold, and not even realize what has been done to their so-called wonder drug. Joe, and myself held up at the park station, since the area was abandoned, there was plenty of food, and supplies for a week. A few days later we heard it over the park station radio, our plan had backfired, the drug was to be used to turn humans into zombies. Every human they injected died instantly. We caused more chaos than damage. How could we have known?

Today we are traveling down a dusty highway in a stolen army truck. Joe, several freedom fighters, and myself have banded together to stop as many of the living dead that we can possibly shoot. Where we are, or what we have become, or where we are heading is unknown, we just shoot at anything that doesn't seem human anymore. As I asked in the beginning, was it worldwide? Maybe so, who knows? As we approach each city, all that is visible, are out of control fires, and smoke. A sure sign that life may not be found in this city either. I wonder what would have become of us, had we not gone out for a peek at the "CITY OF THE DEAD" that night.

Today we live in the world of the dead. Every day that goes by we hope to find another human being, or some sort of life, as we once knew it. Always on the defensive is how we have become accustomed to living. We travel into each city looking for food, weapons, or any needed supplies. We avoid the nights, the zombies seem to see better in the dark, the light affects their coordination. Well, I better wake the guys; we are approaching yet another village, and we have to get our weapons ready. We take turns driving while the others sleep, that is until we approach a village.

I can see smoke at a distance, a sure sign that the living dead have already been here. How did it happen so fast? I keep asking myself, but the world is so ignorant to global catastrophes. We were all so caught up in our own little worlds, that we didn't even realize when a plague, of this magnitude was hitting us, so we were consumed by it. Instead we laid down without a fight, and let it happen. Life depends on us now, death, and violence will be the key to life from this day forward. Our children will know one thing, and one thing only survival of the fittest. Well it's time for target practice, we'll talk soon but for now, if you are reading this letter, you too must be one of the survivors.

THE LAKE PRINT

It was the summer of 2008, not much of a summer this year, there was too much rain, and not enough heat, more like we were having a rainy season. I was taking a walk along Lake Manteno; a beautiful lake surrounded by the city of Manteno nestled deep in the woods of the county. I come out here for a walk every morning before I go to work, nothing beats the morning air, but today was about to change my life forever, along the trail by the lake was what appeared to be a large footprint.

The print was not animal, nor human, it was something in between, something I had never seen before. It was bigger than a size twelve shoe, but not a shoe print at all, it was more like an animal print with three large hoofs, it was deeply pressed in the soil from a lot of weight obviously, but what was it? Here in Manteno there was no wildlife other than deer. A deer hoof print, it simply was not.

I began to examine the print a little further, there were no toes just I guess three large claws on the end. The print was about seven inches wide. The print looked like it came out of the forest, over to the edge of the lake and, then went back into the darkness of the forest. I whatever it was came to the edge for a drink of water. I followed the footprints into the dark forest, just out of curiosity.

At the end of the footprints in the forest, I noticed about six gutted fish laying along side a tree. It appeared that this beast had used the tree to hold the fish, and then slashed them open one by one. What a strange situation, I decided to head back home, and get a camera. A picture of this eerie scene was needed, who would believe me without proof. This footprint had to be seen by the authorities.

I was finally home but I needed more than just a camera, spooked by the print I loaded my handgun, and placed it beneath my beltline, then covered it with my shirt. Here in Illinois there are gun laws, and I surely do not want to end up in the county jail. I began to head back for the short journey to the lake. At last here I was overlooking what use to seem like a quiet, relaxing scene of the lake. Lake Manteno was an eerie sight to walk upon today, who knows what I might encounter living out here now.

Today that picture seemed different, as the lake appeared gloomy and, desolate. The ripple of the waves on the lake seemed to bring in a sudden burst of fear in the air. Something was out here, and today was different than any other walk along the lake. I even felt spooked, like something was watching me. I took a few photos, then made my way back into the forest to track this beast, or whatever made the tracks. All of a sudden storm clouds moved in, and then it began to pour down rain, sending me on my way home.

I gave up the hunt and, made my way back home to get ready for work. I spoke to no one at work about the prints; they would have thought I was crazy anyway. At work I stared at the clock waiting for quitting time to arrive, it seemed like every minute was an hour today. I couldn't wait to go back out to the lake for more clues as to what made the strange prints, along the shore of Lake Manteno this morning.

After lunch one of my co-workers was talking about a murder near the lake that happened last night sometime. What a coincidence, especially after I spotted the print. He had heard over the radio that a body was discovered, mutilated, and what appeared to be an animal tracks surrounding the body. I began to wonder if the prints I saw this morning were to blame for the strange murder that happened last night.

Immediately I called the sheriffs department to ask if they had matched footprints to any known species. The local sheriff began to question me, then asked me to come down to the station for more questions. I began to wonder if calling in, was a bad idea to begin with, what if they thought I had something to do with this grisly murder. I could show the police the pictures of the prints I took, but what would they think, why was this guy out here with a camera?

Once at the station I introduced myself to Officer Rodriguez, hello my name is Elliott, this morning I was walking along the Lake Manteno, as I do every morning before work, when I noticed some strange footprints along the shore. Tell me! This body you found was it slashed open, with what appeared to be claw marks? Immediately the sheriff stated, "how do you know that?" I replied "because I followed the prints into the forest and, came upon some gutted fish, the same way you described the body, that was found."

Officer Rodriguez began to look at me as if I was now a suspect, but I told him, hey, look on this camera! I have pictures that I took of some strange prints by the lake. Yes we found animal tracks near the scene, he replied. "Animal tracks!" I said "you call a print this big with only three hoofs, an animal? What kind of animal sheriff? I asked. The sheriff told me to go home and let him do the investigating, "I'll keep in touch," he replied; just leave your information with the front desk officer on your way out.

I headed home, but as I drove by the lake I could see the flashing lights of an ambulance, and several police cars at the location along the lake. Another victim obviously, I wondered if I should pull over and have a look, or wait until later that evening, to check it out for myself. So there I was pulling over to the side of the road, and making my way through the forest to the lake area.

Then I saw it, the ambulance driver was on the floor mutilated from head to toe, covered in blood. What could have done this? I proceeded to find the police officers, when all of a sudden I heard several shots fired, then I heard a thunderous roar! I heard the screams of the two frightened souls, as this creature was tearing them apart right before my very own eyes.

There it was seven feet tall with tree trunks for arms, and legs all covered with leaves. It had jaws with razor sharp teeth, and a green mossy appearance. Was this a tree monster, the mythological creature called the Dryad? I slowly stepped backwards to get out of here fast. I must have stepped on a branch, because I heard it snap, and this thing turned, and looked directly at me. The creature let out a loud roar, and dashed back into the wooded area. How lucky I was, I thought.

Petrified at what just took place, I did not know what to do, I walked over to the police car, and got on the radio, help, help officers are down, I shouted "send help to Lake Manteno fast," I cried. "Soon the area was filled with squad cars. There I was staring at the barrel of several guns, all I could hear was "get on the floor, now!" I of course complied, "wait! You guys don't think I did this, do you?" I replied. There I was in the back seat of a police car on my way to jail. Officer Rodriguez just stared as they brought me in, I heard him say, "I knew we should have arrested that clown earlier."

So here I am doing time in a musty jail cell, while a Dryad runs wild in the Manteno Lake area. No more reports have come in, and the creature was never sighted again. Why did this creature stop his rampage? Who would believe me now? Heed my warning stay away from Lake Manteno, in the wee hours of the morning, for out of the mist, you too may fall victim to the tree monster of Manteno. I know he's still out there somewhere in the dense fog.

The police said the large prints that were found in the area around the murdered bodies, had to be my footprints. I was blamed for the murder of several people, a cover up no doubt. The police said they were baffled as to how I did it. To this day the forensic officers are still trying to piece it together, how a man could have ripped out the throats of all the victims. If the police would only for once in their stubborn minds listen to people, they might solve some simple crimes. The police failed to check my camera, for on that very camera was the proof I needed to set me free, on that camera was, THE LAKE PRINT.

GHOST HOUSE

Hello, my name is Todd and I search the country for old houses, and sometimes-haunted houses. I take pictures for my magazine, they buy the best photos, and that's how I earn a living. I was eating at a diner in a town called Momence; I was just passing through on my way to Chicago. That's when I overheard it; a young couple was ranting about the disappearance of some friends to the local sheriff, in an old house not far away. I had a few days before my deadline, so I decided to check this one out for myself. Little did I know I would soon come face to face with evil.

The town was Hopkins Park a country location buried in Kankakee County. It was here that the legend began; I was investigating supernatural happenings when I came upon the ghost house of Hopkins Park. A home located on the edge of town on a hill overlooking the main road. The house was dark gray, with old broken shutters. The porch was the width of the home. Creepy windows, and tall grass in front yard gave the home a wicked appearance. I work for Ghost Magazine; my job was to take pictures of supposedly haunted houses for our quarterly cover. I had never run into a haunted house before. This house was different it seemed to call you inside, at first glance.

The house was too eerie to explore, I just wanted to take a few pictures and leave. On this day my life was about to change, the house was alive. I stood in front of the house and took a picture, when all of a sudden the front door burst into pieces. I ran back to my car, and drove back to the office. I got a team together from Paranormal Magazine, and we went back to the house in Hopkins Park. When we arrived at the house the front door was still standing, and of course the guys didn't believe me. We decided to stay for a while, and explore this Ghost House. It soon began to rain outside, and it turned gloomy. The front door slammed shut, and the lights began to flicker.

I went upstairs to take some pictures, in the hallway ghostly faces appeared in the wood screaming, "help me." I called the guys upstairs but as soon as they hit the stairway the stairs began to melt, the guys were swallowed up by the house. I continued to take pictures, then all of a sudden the windows burst into pieces, as lightning, and thunder roared outside. I had to get out, I tried to jump downstairs, but it was too far, and the lights flickering created a strobe light appearance. Then it was silent for a minute the house was back to normal. I ran down the stairs, heading for the basement to see what had become of the guys that accompanied me. The basement was misty, and dark. I saw again the faces of ghostly apparitions reaching out for me from the walls.

The house was certainly haunted, but what had happened to these lost souls in the walls. The house was some sort of evil entity that took the living to a world beyond. The only thing they could do was ask for help. I had to get out, forget my friends, they can find their own way out. I climbed the stairs that led from the cellar to the kitchen. I tried the back door, but it was locked tight. I looked out the windows to see if the rain had stopped. It was not even wet outside, why? Then a face appeared from the floor, it was moaning, then said, "stay away from the stairway! It is the mouth of this demon." I knew then my friends were doomed, I had to get out.

Then I heard a loud voice coming from the basement, it said, "gettt ouuttt!" in a chilling voice. I saw the front door bolt open, so I made a run for it. I was about to get in my car, but I turned to get one last picture of the Ghost House. I drove a few blocks away then I stopped the car then got out, and stared at the house from a distance. Its funny from here the two upper windows were lit, the house seemed to have eyes from a distance. I could see that the rain, and thunder were only visible around this Ghost House.

I drove back to the office, to develop the film.

I was still wondering what I was going to tell the police about the two guys who are still at the house. I didn't want to be locked up in an asylum for the insane. The picture I took as I was leaving that day, told the story, for in that picture were my two friends. The faces, and their hands reaching out is all that was visible in the picture coming from the front door. The Ghost House had taken two more souls. I could always show the picture to someone, but who would believe it? If you want to see a haunted house, take a drive to Hopkins Park, It will be your last.

ATTIC EYES

It was the fall of 1987; I was riding my bicycle to school passing the old Jones mansion, a creepy old Victorian home on Center Avenue in Bradley. I rode passed it every day on the way to school in the morning. The villager's thought the house was haunted, strange things were said to happen at this creepy old house, I think it was just because it looked scary, that the town was afraid of the house. Often one could hear a story being told by a campfire, about this old house. One time even aliens were thought to occupy the home. The stories about the house go on and on, with no real evidence to support any of these occurrences.

School was out, and it was time to get out of this brick fortress here at BBCHS. I couldn't wait for the bell to ring at 3 O clock. There I was riding home from school, hello my name is Jerri Fout, the day was cloudy, looks like a storm was brewing, so I had to get home. There it was the old Jones mansion, I just glanced as I rode past it. Then all of a sudden I saw it; a set of fiery red eyes, were staring at me from the attic window of the creepy old house. What was it? I soon became a believer, was the house haunted? I stopped, and peered upward at the creepy mansion. Sure enough it was a set of eyes staring back at me, it started to rain, so I began to make my way home.

I was finally home, so I went over to see if I should tell my dad, he would believe me, my dad was an author of horror stories. My dad wrote many books on things like this, maybe he could tell me the history, of this haunted house. My dad said the house had a history of ghosts, but he believed the stories were told to scare kids away from the empty home. I didn't even mention it to him after that, I started to walk out the door to get a closer look at the eyes that stared back at me today, from the attic of the old house on Center Avenue in Bradley. It was dark out, and the moon was glistening over the village. The kind of night you saw in a horror movie.

As I was approaching the haunted house, I rode my bike around the back of the house, I had to remain undetected, or someone might call the police if they saw me snooping about. The attic windows were visible from the back of the house, and there they were again, a set of fiery red eyes. The eyes were staring directly at me, and then they disappeared into the darkness. I tried the back door, and it was locked. I was determined to see what it was, so I smashed a window, and crawled inside the eerie house, on Center Avenue. Once inside I began to look around for anything that seemed out of place. I saw a huge spiral staircase that led upstairs into darkness.

I began to wonder if I should go upstairs, or leave. Then I heard it! something was moving about in the upstairs hallway. The ghost of dead souls I thought, no, it couldn't be. I had to know what was haunting this old house. I began to make my way upstairs, following the spiral rail that led to, possibly my demise. It sure was dark, and cobwebs filled the ceiling. After a brief search of the upstairs, I proceeded to go up into the attic. The fiery red eyes came from the attic windows anyway. This must be it, a creepy old ladder led up to an opening in the ceiling.

I started to make my way up the beaten ladder that housed the eerie ghost in the attic. The secret to the haunting was about to be discovered. Then I heard a noise, something jumped away from one of the attic windows. It was coming towards me slowly in the darkness, I began to wonder if I should cut, and run. Then a familiar voice came from below "meow!" it was a black cat! The mystery was solved. The fiery red eyes that stared at people from a distance, was a trapped cat in the attic. Little did this furry feline know, but he was to blame for the ghost that frightened the neighborhood on Center Avenue, in Bradley. I took the little guy home with me; the ghost of Center Avenue now lives on Lasalle Avenue in Bradley.

THE CREEPER

In the fall of 1987 we moved into a secluded farmhouse in St. Anne. The house was located in the country, without any neighbors for miles. A creek ran through the property that trickled along side of an old structure, thought to be slave quarters in the 1940s. A home filled with history, and beauty, and in the country what a great setting. Hello, my name is Edina, and we just bought this old house, my husband and I are looking to settle here for a long time to come. These old houses are hard to come by, and what a deal we got here in St. Anne. Three weeks have gone by, and we are finally finished moving into our new country home.

One day I was out in the backyard hanging some clothes, when I heard a strange noise coming from the slave quarters. I began to look at the place from a distance, wondering if it was a small animal shuffling about on the roof. I saw the shadow of a cloaked figure from a distance; I do not believe he saw me. What was he looking for? It appeared as if he was searching for something. I ran back to the house, and called the police. Officer Scalise arrived at the scene, and checked out the slave quarters. "I did not find anything misplaced, or broken into," he replied. Ok "thanks anyway" I responded.

Officer Scalise said, "What did this Creeper look like?" Creeper! I said, what gave you any indication he was a Creeper?

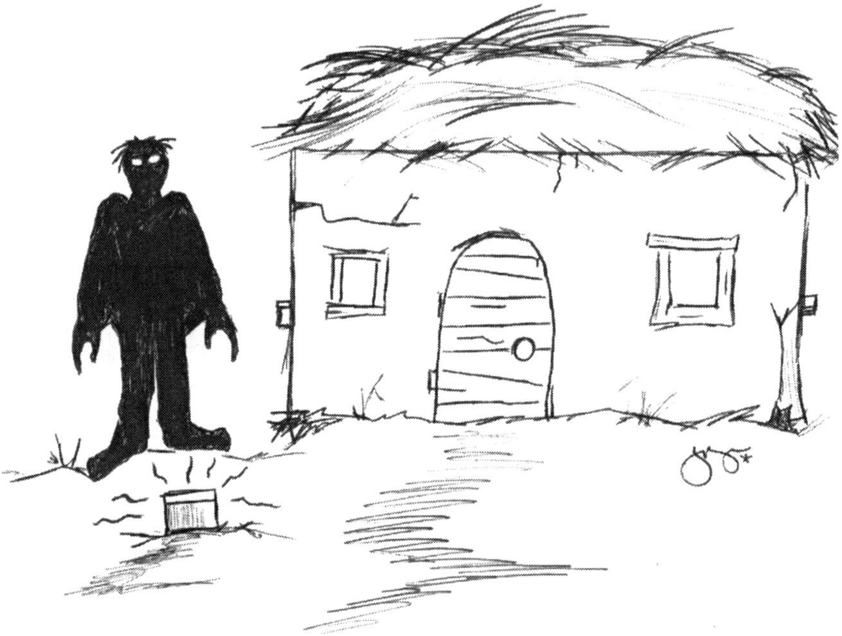

The officer said, "there is a legend in these parts, about a man that was hung, and his eyes were removed". Many people in these parts have seen this ghost, and they named him the Creeper. They say he is looking for his eyes; every tenant that lives here has spotted a man dressed in a black cloak, with no eyes. I, of course have never seen this Creeper, as they call him here in town. Be careful if you see anything again don't hesitate to call us. The local policeman seemed sort of scared to be here, it was getting dark, and he kept staring at the slave quarters, and at the darkening sky. He seemed to want to leave before it got dark.

My husband showed up, and I explained to him what the day brought. He said, "lets go out there and see what we can find." We entered the slave quarters, and boy was it a mess, it looked like it had not been opened in a hundred years. "Nothing here" said my husband, so we locked it back up, and went back home, I found several books that I brought with me. Later that night I began to browse through the books, one of the books looked like a diary. The diary told the story of a young man who was in love with the plantation owner's daughter. It appeared they were having an affair, but the father, and the villagers put a stop to it.

This diary seemed to be written by the mother of this young man. The young man was beaten, hung, and they carved his eyes out in front of the woman he was in love with, and then burned him alive. I began to wonder how tragic that sight might have been for a mother to witness. It was getting late; I took a glance through the window at the slave quarters one more time. I noticed again a light was on in the slave quarters. How can this be there was no electricity out there! Then I saw him again a cloaked figure moving about inside. This time he came out of the slave quarters, and stared directly at me.

I came outside to get a better look at this intruder. This time I got a good look at this Creeper he appeared to have bright lights for his eye sockets. Then he ran into the forest, and disappeared into the night. The question seemed to be, where were his eyes? Did the villagers keep them? I had to find out, this lost soul was not out to harm anyone. I believe he was just wandering the earth in search of his eyes. Maybe he wanted revenge on anyone who lived on the property. I had to find out, either way. The next day I visited the local library, in search of some answers to my questions. I found nothing, and no one in town admitted to knowing anything about the incident.

I stopped by the police station to ask Officer Scalise about the diary. The officer said the book was a childish prank, to scare kids to sleep. I told him, "that sounds fair, but I have seen this Creeper twice!" the officer said I needed to be careful; it may be a thief looking for something to steal, yeah right! The whole town was in on it, and they were frightened to mention anything about what had happened on that gloomy day of injustice. It appeared that every one connected with the Creeper, was a relative of this crime. The town was hiding the secret out of fear. The Creeper was haunting them for their sins.

I went back home and began to finish the diary, inside was a photograph of the crime. The villagers must have taken it for the old woman to remember, how sad. This picture was a clue. In the photograph was a small red box, next to the corpse. I'll bet that's where the eyes were hidden. Where was the red box? Upon further reading I discovered the curse to the town, it was in the diary, it read "my son will haunt you for your sins, and only I can stop him." The villagers did not carve his eyes out, but his mother did, and used this evil, to scare the villagers. The mother died, and now he cannot rest until his eyes are found. That's why he's been spotted on the plantation grounds; the Creeper is looking for his eyes.

I started to think where would a woman hide something very precious to her? Underneath her mattress! I bolted out the door to the slave quarters, and begin to look in between the mattresses, and sure enough, there it was. The small red box was covered in dust from the aging years, I was afraid to open it. I decided that I would let the Creeper do it, I waited for darkness to fall, and then I set the box on a large rock near the entrance of the slave quarters. The Creeper appeared out of the misty night, he looked straight at me; I was on my porch staring back at him. He opened the box, then stared at me for a minute then waved at me with one hand, and then a flash of light is all I saw, then he was gone.

I have not seen the Creeper since that day, and I still have people in the town asking me how we can stay at this house, with a ghost creeping around. I just smile, they don't have to know, and who would believe me anyway. I had the slave quarters torn down, and we planted a garden over the area. The local police continue to patrol my area at night, out of guilt no doubt. When the townsfolk ask me about the Creeper, I just tell them "yes I still see the Creeper at night." It keeps the town people away from our country home. I believe the Creeper of St. Anne is still alive in the minds of our small town, so people continue to report seeing him.

"We'll you've made it this far huh? Then look in the closet.

THE WEREWOLF OF BRADLEY

Hello my name is Jesse; let me tell you a story that is eating away at me, and no one cares to believe me. The whole town is looking for a werewolf in the village Bradley. People have been mutilated, ripped apart, and torn from limb, to limb. They say there is a large wolf here in the village, and on a full moon, a werewolf can be heard howling in the village of Bradley. The local newspaper dismisses the stories, even though the howling can be heard all the way to Momence. The police still do not have any leads on the strange mutilations, caused by the werewolf. Without suspects or clues, how can this creature be caught? The city detectives need to look at the ancient legends of Tibet, and the killer will be found, but who wants to believe in werewolves today? Obviously no one, how many more will die before they piece it together?

Last month, a team of dogs, were dispatched after an old couple was found mutilated on Grand Avenue. It was late one night when the police got a call about a wolf howling in the alley on Grand Avenue. The police arrived at the scene, only to find the house on Grand Avenue in shambles; the front door was torn off its hinges by something very strong. The occupants were found dead on arrival, too messy to mention. Large wolf tracks were spotted leaving the premises, so the police K-9 unit was dispatched. The tracks led them to a secluded factory down the street, but the dogs followed by the police were found the next morning eaten, and ripped apart. The murders continue, and the authorities are still baffled. On a full moon night you can always bet, the howling will begin, and another victim will be sacrificed to the Bradley Werewolf.

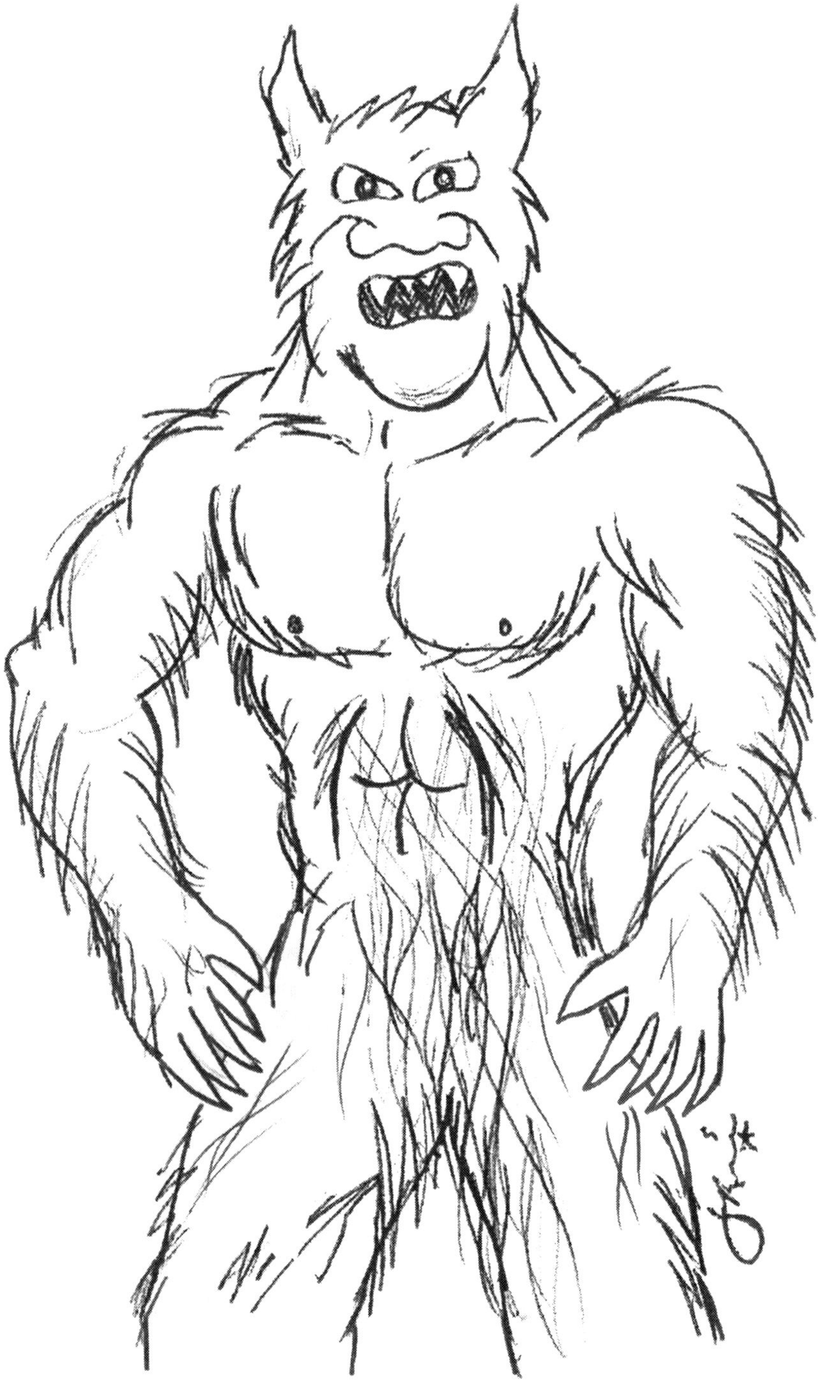

The gossip in the village is that a large predator is responsible, not a human being. The Bradley villagers still go about their business, until the moon is full that is, then extra police units patrol the village. The Werewolf is too crafty for the police, he is thought to be in too many places at the same time, I believe everything seen in the shadows like a cat, or raccoon is thought to be the beast of the night. The gloominess of the evening keeps the citizens awake on moonlit nights, people armed with handguns in their own back yards, are visible from patrolling squad cars. The whole werewolf craze has consumed the law enforcement community. The police have their hands full with gun toting fools, and 911 calls that are alarmed by every noise, on moonlit nights, making it even easier for this wolfman to roam at large undetected.

Although no one has ever seen the beast, many have claimed to have survived altercations with the wolfman. The beast, last weekend broke into a mans garage, and walked unsuspectedly into a trap, because the man and his friends were waiting for him, they shot him four times, but not with a silver bullet, the wolfman bolted from the garage, and the men gave chase. The men, who are now deceased, tried to pursue the injured creature, but the men only met their death, at the hands of the Bradley Werewolf.

The beast pulled one of the victim's chests wide open, the other two ran, but were chased down, and eaten. One report said the wolfman chased a woman in a car; the beast lunged onto the vehicle and raked his claws on the hood, and that is all that was found on the vehicle, the woman's body was not recovered. The Wolfman is getting closer to the downtown area when he searches for his meals. I think the overpopulation, of the village and the crowds that walk the night, camouflage his appearance from a distance. A werewolf in Bradley, I never would have guessed it myself.

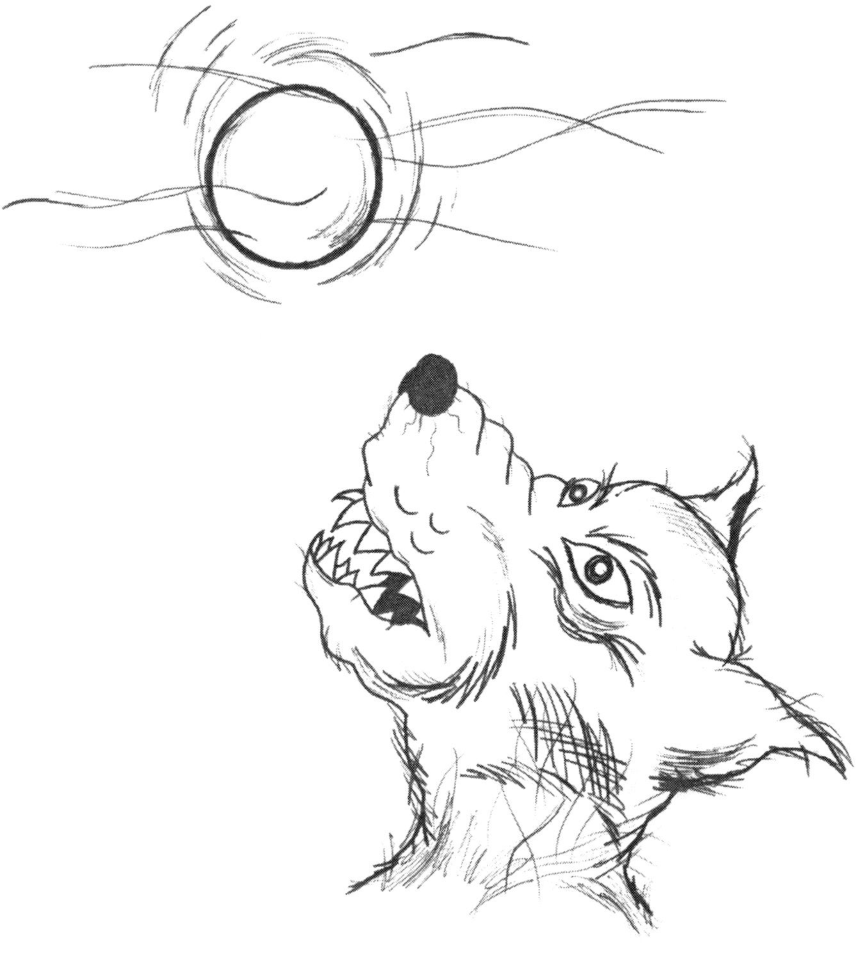

The other day I took a walk by the Kankakee River, and of course the moon was full. I was hoping this wolfman was not in the area, but I was mistaken. A loud howling was coming from a distance, and then I heard the heavy breathing of this creature, immediately a man screamed in horror. I ran up to a nearby tree, but all I could see from the reflection on the river that was somewhat of a blur, was a large hairy head, which stood on two legs, massive arms with big claws, it seemed to look straight at me, but it could not see me. I saw the beast picked the man up like a rag doll, then the wolfman ripped into his throat, and he ate peacefully by the river, like he belonged there. I made my way back home quickly; I didn't report it either, why? Let the beast dine in peace, I thought.

Today is October 31st, and another full moon will rise in about an hour. I wonder how many hapless fools, will become dinner tonight for the Wolfman of Bradley. The weather is perfect, and the day is Halloween, what a perfect night for deception, and murder, the police will not even know where to look. Many people will howl tonight, and many will be dressed, as wolfmen, and many drunken fools will think they are wolfmen, ha! The night calls for the creatures of the night, so beware, stay indoors tonight, because it will not be safe with a full-grown werewolf roaming the village of Bradley tonight. The innocent victims will get their last breath on Halloween night, and the last thing they will see is a set of red fiery eyes, and the fangs that will tear them apart.

I have said enough, it's almost time for the moon to rise, and in a few minutes a large werewolf will stalk the village of Bradley, and there isn't a thing anyone can do about it! The trick or treaters better beware, for a snack on the way sounds good to the wolfman of Bradley. You are probably wondering why I know so much, about the sightings, in detail, when before I mentioned that no one has ever seen this beast. I Jesse, no need to mention last names, can tell you that I was there each time it happened. I have seen this beast that escapes everyone, I saw my reflection in the water near the river one night. Well, it's time to go because in a few minutes I will have to feed, the moon is calling me, and my hands are starting to grow hair, it's almost dinner time, lock your doors tonight, and keep your children home, because tonight, I will be the shadow in the darkness, that stalks you in the moonlight.

DEMON PIT

There's a small town nestled deep in the country off highway 17 west, called Irwin. I grew up there as a boy, about twenty years ago. The small town was good country living at the time. Today I have finished college, and I am coming home, to my parent's house. My parents have passed away, leaving me the house that I longed to forget. At the time I was about to start college some strange disappearances began, in the town of Irwin. I had left just when the craziness begun. All I could do was read about it in the newspapers, and sometimes my parents would tell me what little gossip they knew. The demons were loose in Irwin.

There was an old graveyard behind the local church. The villagers say the church was not always a church, but something different. In that cemetery was a gravestone that read, Demon Pit. The grave was covered with a large rock, but there was not thought to be a body buried there, just an entrance to hell, so the villagers covered it up then posted the gravestone warning. The gravestone warning read, "Beware for underneath lies the bottomless pit, which houses the dark ones, do not open!" Of course some fool had to be curious, and remove the rock, now the night becomes the slaying ground for the demons in Irwin.

The villagers fear the night, for that's when they come out of the Demon Pit. What are they you ask? They are hells slaves, sent to torment the village. The maroon figures with glass eyes seem to be tormenters, not murderers. No one has been killed; they just come up missing probably from moving, or running for their lives, and not returning to their homes, who knows. Some say the demons pull their victims down the passageway to hell. I have heard too many stories to know what is true. Why torment us you ask? The man that occupied the property long ago, of what is now a church was said to be a Warlock.

Long ago a Warlock was said to inhabit the village of Irwin. This man was an undertaker, that's why there is a graveyard behind the church today. The Warlock was said to experiment on the dead, bringing them back to life. After a funeral, the villagers would watch him dig up the graves, and carry the dead back to the funeral home. Fed up with this illegal practice, some of the villagers gathered one night for vengeance. The villagers burned down the funeral home, and stoned the Warlock to death, but not before he cursed them. The Warlock chanted, "I will send my legions to torment you for this crime against me." The Warlock then died; afterwards the townspeople built a church over the funeral home to forget about the nightmare in Irwin.

The day the Warlock was to be buried, the body was missing from his casket. It was later discovered that there was a deep hole in his backyard, with footprints leading to it. Some say the Warlock got up and walked to his own grave, deep in hell. The villagers believed this was a gateway to hell, so they covered up the hole with a huge rock, and posted a warning on the gravestone. Over a hundred years have passed, and a graveyard was built around the gravestone. The legend says someone removed the stone, exposing the gateway for the demons to come out, at the witching hour each night.

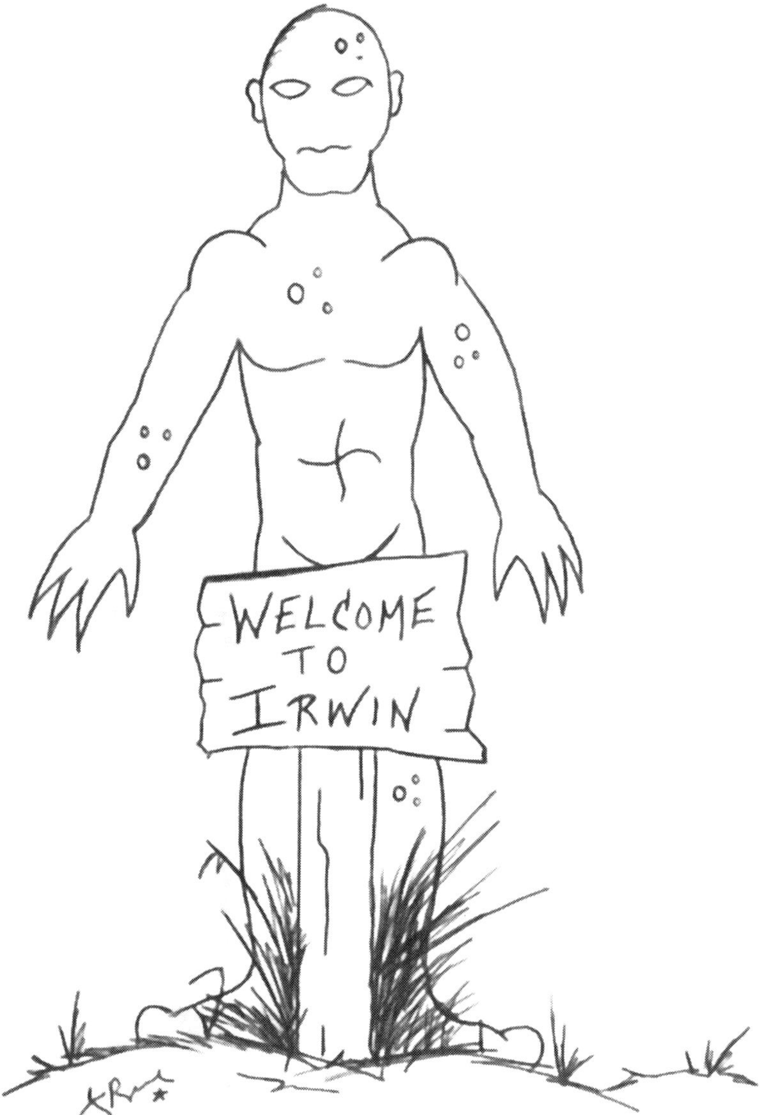
WELCOME
TO
IRWIN

Tonight I have to stay the night at my parent's house, where the church can be seen from a distance. I hope the stories are not true. I was tired from the trip so I went straight to bed. Later that night I was awaken by the sound of screams in the night, a little after midnight. I looked out from my bedroom window only to discover a woman running from what appeared to be a dark figure, moaning in agony. I had to help her; I jumped out of bed, and gave chase to this prowler. I got close enough to see the eyes were like transparent glass. Was this one of the demons, that people were reporting? I struck the being with a shovel. The demon fell to his grave; he did not get up, and then out of nowhere the ground swallowed the demon up. The girl was nowhere to be found.

I decided to take a walk over to the gravesite, to see what was coming out of this demon pit. The graveyard was very spooky, the trees seemed to be reaching for me as the wind blew the branches back, and forth. There it was, what an eerie site to see, the deep pit that was to blame for this demons appearance. I looked down at the dark pit, it seemed bottomless, the sounds of teeth gnashing, and moans of pain could be heard, what an awful feeling it was. The scent of death was in the air, I had to find a way to cover the pit once again. I got in my car and slammed into the huge rock pushing it over the demon pit. I hoped the nightmare was over, and then I went back to bed. The next morning I sold the home, and moved to Bradley.

It's been over twenty years, and I have not heard of anymore-strange demon sightings since that eerie night. I began to wonder if the rock was keeping the demons at bay. I once believed in God, but I can say I now believe in Satan also. The town of Irwin has a dark secret, hidden in that graveyard behind the local church. If you happen to wander into Irwin, stay away from the graveyard. I don't know if some fool has removed the stone since that dark night. A demon may be waiting for you in the mist. Evil has a new name, and it comes out of the ground at midnight, in the town of Irwin.

FIREWOOD

It was the summer of 2007; we were headed out of town for a camping trip to a small wooded area in Salina Township, in Illinois. A small wooded village nestled in a quiet location with a small population. The perfect spot for camping, or to relax and enjoy the peacefulness of the great outdoors. We hit the open road leaving the village of Bradley, for a three-day weekend in the great outdoors. Camping is the one vacation we look forward to all year long. All winter long I picture the very sight of an open fire along a river, or lake. I am just waiting for the weather to break, so we can enjoy the distinct sounds of nature, and calm night in the woods.

There it was, the Star Campground along a river, B-64 was our reserved spot, and it was perfect. The site was on a hill overlooking a raging river. I quickly began to set up the area before nightfall, as my wife Shirley set up the tent. A few hours later we decided to take a ride through the small village to explore some of the sights to see, if there were any that is. Then all of a sudden, Shirley said "Jesse! We forgot to bring firewood!" That's ok, I'll stop at the local camp store on our way out, but they did not sell firewood at all, Charlie the storeowner said, "just follow the signs on the roads, there are many places that sell firewood in the back roads Salina."

We set off for the main dirt road that led us to the campground, and sure enough, on a utility pole were several signs depicting the sale of firewood. We followed one of the signs about two miles away from the campsite. The sign led to another hand written sign that pointed another way saying, "firewood next left" so there we went again, until we came upon a run down farmhouse on the left side of the dirt road. It was pretty hidden from the campsite, a sign next to the mailbox on the road, read, "firewood for sale." It appeared kind of spooky, and eerie as the dirt path led to a small camp store in a trailer home, but the firewood signs led to the back of the house next to a large barn.

The barn looked like one of those strange places you see only in a horror movie. I looked around for a minute afraid to get out of my vehicle, when out of nowhere an old lady was standing next to my passenger window with a basket of kittens, she startled us. The old woman asked my wife if she wanted to buy a kitten. We said "no!" we are looking for firewood! Got any? But the old woman made her way back into the barn in silence. How strange we thought, then at that very moment a face appeared out from the barn, slightly waving us inside then vanishing back inside very quickly. Shirley said, "You're not going in there are you?"

I hesitated for a moment, then I thought how silly we were acting, what could possibly go wrong; maybe they are just strange people. At that very moment another car pulled into the drive, a light blue blazer, and stopped at the camp store near the entrance of the farmhouse, and started beeping their horn. The strange couple made their way to the camp store near the front of the farmhouse, one carrying a bloody machete. They just stared at us; as we were petrified in our vehicle. I told Shirley "lets take a peek inside?" Ok responded Shirley. We got out of the vehicle, and went inside the eerie barn, inside the barn was a gutted goat on a table, freshly cut, and dripping blood on the barn floor. On the wall of the barn were many different styles of machetes, some soaked with blood, but why? I saw that near the back of the opposite wall in the barn, was what appeared to be shackles bolted to the wall, with arm, and leg irons, and next to them a buckets of bloody body parts, from whomever was there before us, no doubt.

This was too strange; we immediately dashed for the door, got into our vehicle, and drove away as fast as possible leaving nothing but dust in our escape. I jumped the curve rather than wait for the vehicle to move that was in front of the camp store trailer. Shirley, and I were not going to wait, we don't want to know what happens if you get trapped inside that eerie barn. The scene in the barn felt too weird, and out of place. What were they doing in the barn to innocent unknown victims was our question. I did not see one log of firewood inside that barn, but the signs that read "firewood" pointed to the barn, an obvious trap, no doubt.

We decided to illegally cut down some firewood at the campsite; I always brought my hand axe when camping just in case. The fire was set, then we sat down in front of the flames to reflect on what we had just seen, or were we just too paranoid from watching too many horror movies? At that very moment a couple of teenagers walked over to our campsite. The two teens a boy, and a girl in their worried state asked us if we had seen their parents. The boy said his parents went to look for firewood several hours ago, and they had not yet returned. I said, "Where did they go for firewood?" The girl responded, "We don't know, we believe they just followed the street signs."

I asked the troubled teens, what color was your parent's vehicle? They responded light blue! Immediately myself, and Shirley turned and looked at each other, because we knew we had seen the light blue blazer, at the firewood trailer site, earlier today, where we sped away like bats out of hell, in fear of what may become of us. One could only imagine what had happened to their parents; maybe they were chained to the wall, or gutted like the goat on the table, who knows. I was not going to tell the teens anything, I just told them to call the police, and have them check out the firewood sites. Out there somewhere in the secluded woods of Salina Township, lies a deep horrifying cannibalistic couple who just can't wait, to sell you FIREWOOD.

THE BRADLEY CHUPACABRA

It was the summer of 1989, a somewhat disoriented global year, not too much sun this year, and a cool breeze surrounded the village this season. Hello my name is Wyatt, and I was taking a walk home from the local fruit market on Route 50. I started walking along Brookmont Boulevard heading west. I reached the railroad tracks, and decided to walk along the tracks to get to my home on Dearborn Avenue in Bradley. There I was balancing myself as I walked on the railway grid along the forested area on the side of the beaten path that led into darkness between the highway, and the housing complex in Bradley.

I could hear the sounds of nature surround me, then all of a sudden I heard a loud scream, and then it was totally quiet, and not even the birds could be heard. How strange that, all the sounds of nature seemed to stop, what made this awful noise, and then I heard it again, what was it? All of a sudden I began to notice blood drip on the ground beside me, I took a quick glance upwards and, there it was, what was it? It appeared to be eating a squirrel, it was about four foot tall, with small horns along it's spine, huge black eyes, razor sharp talons, along with blood drenched teeth, out of fear, I took a few steps backwards into the brush.

I had to get home, but how, I was afraid to move, or startle this creature, it may attack me. I watched as it devoured the squirrel until it was gone. This creature had finally finished its meal, and then grasped a tree leaped into the air, and disappeared into the forest. I followed the train tracks back to my neighborhood, and then made my way home. I had to tell somebody, but who would believe me? At home, I went straight to my computer, and got on the Internet, I found out, that this was the famed Chupacabra, the flying goatsucker of Puerto Rico, but what was it doing here in Bradley? This small creature was said to inhabit the jungles of Puerto Rico, not North America.

There in Puerto Rico this creature was responsible for the many deaths of goats, and small sheep in the densely forested jungle villages. These creatures were known to attack from above, and lunge their teeth into the backside of their victims, and then drain them of all their blood. Wow! But here in Bradley? How is that possible I asked myself? I made my way back through the brush near the railway tracks; I had to get a picture with my camera. I set off to for search the famed Chupacabra, I took a peek with my binoculars through the trees, and there it was. The Bradley Chupacabra was perched atop the highest tree in the small forest between the railway tracks, and Brookmont Boulevard.

I could see the creature had green scaly skin, and moved about like a swift squirrel from tree, to tree. It was moving too fast for me to snap a shot, almost as if it knew, when I was going to take its picture. I began to follow it though the forest, but the creature spotted me! I was petrified, it turned its head back, and forth as it gazed at me through the trees, and I could only see the glare of the sun, as it blinded me when I looked upwards at the little beast. Then I lost it, where did it go so fast, I asked? All of a sudden I heard a yelping sound, like a dog maybe, and yes sure enough, a few feet away a dog was the next victim of the Bradley Chupacabra. The Chupacabra had lunged down on a helpless dog, and began to drink its blood. I got out of the woods as fast as I could run.

Then next day one of my neighbors was missing, police were combing the area for a man, and his dog. I began to wonder if the Chupacabra was to blame for the disappearances, should I say something to the police? Maybe I would be questioned, no! Who would believe me anyway? I decided to talk to old man Rodriguez, who lived at the end of our block, a strange old timer that was thought to be crazy, for his beliefs in the occult, and black magic. Old man

Rodriguez knew exactly what the Chupacabra was, and suggested we trap it. We got in his old pick up truck, and headed to the farm surplus store a few miles away.

On the way to the farm surplus store, old man Rodriguez said we should wait a few days until everything is back to normal. I said, "Will a trap hold it?" he replied, "of course, I have seen many of these little demons in my day; they are quite crafty, but not at all strong". Once at the store we looked for a suitable trap for the little terror. We bought a large trap, and then headed back to his house to plan our capture. What should we use for bait, I asked? A gutted, and mutilated opossum, old man Rodriguez replied, the blood will summon him. Three days went by, and we were ready for the little beast in the dark of night, so we set off for the small forest behind our houses. Old man Rodriguez set the trap in the woods, and we just waited for the creature to come, and dine.

WARNER BRIDGE

The Chupacabra made his screeching scream then began to make his way towards the steel cage that was awaiting his capture. The creature looked around for a few quick seconds, and then made its way into the trap, as we peered from the distant brush. Then it happened the creature took the bait, and the trap closed! The Chupacabra began to wear himself out by smacking himself back, and forth until he finally gave up. Old man Rodriguez had secured a rope to the cage; and then we pulled it over to his pickup truck, then covered it up with a tarp, and headed out of town for his release.

As we began to drive out of town, I said, "why not call the police?" old man Rodriguez replied, "this creature is not ready for the world to see, and the world is not ready for this creature either, we must set it free, and let it survive where it cannot be seen, nor heard, somewhere densely wooded, and secluded". We stopped along a wooded area on Warner Bridge road, near the State Park. I got out of the vehicle, and followed old man Rodriguez to a densely wooded area. Old man Rodriguez unlatched the cage, and set the creature loose, then we watched as this incredible creature took to the trees, and disappeared into the woods. It's been twenty years since that day, and every now and then, I read about campers that come up missing in the Warner Bridge area, the local newspaper reports the disappearances as unknown, but only I, know the truth. So every time I drive past Warner Bridge road, I slow my vehicle down just enough, hoping to catch a glimpse, of the famed creature from South America, called The Chupacabra.

CLAWS

It was the winter of 2009, on this cold November night the wind had picked up, and the temperature began to drop, a snowstorm was predicted for the city of Kankakee, the winter nights in our city were always unpredictable, if the weather station called for snow, then we would probably get a snowstorm, or icy rain. The winter season could not be predicted here in Kankakee. As I looked outside, I saw the snowflakes were getting bigger, and the wind was getting stronger. Visibility was dangerous for traveling motorist; this was not a night for anyone to be out in. The winter night was treacherous yet peaceful, most of the city was home sitting in front of their fireplaces, like I was tonight.

I lived in a two-story farmhouse on Grinnell Road; my living room was upstairs overlooking the Kankakee valley, and what a beautiful sight to see, overlooking the entire lighted community on stormy nights like tonight. I was tucked in front of my fireplace, with my cat Midnight right beside me, she too was frightened by the weather this cold

November night. My wife was tucked in bed, it was about 1:30 in the morning and no one was up but me, so it seemed. My name is J.R. and as I turned on the television, I noticed the cable was out, so I turned on the radio instead to see how much snow the storm was about to dump on us tonight.

The weather man predicted six inches, and below zero weather for the next few days. I pulled the recliner over to the window to watch the snowstorm pummel the city. There's nothing more beautiful than snow falling on a cold blistery night. Then I saw it! A large white figure was in the neighbor's backyard. What was it? I could hear the neighbor's dogs barking like crazy. I took a second glance maybe it was someone in a white fur coat. Then I saw it again, what a strange figure it was taller than the neighbors six foot fence, I still could not get a good look because of the blowing snow. Then all of a sudden I heard a loud roar, all the dogs stopped barking, and my cat stood up, and ran away.

I went and got my binoculars, oh my gosh, what was it? A Yeti? What was an abominable snowman doing in Kankakee? The large creature starred directly up at me, as it took a bite out of the neighbor's dog, and then ran away into the night. I immediately called the police, but they laughed at me, and said "we'll send a squad over when we can, we don't want to tie up any of the officers over monsters in the snow," OK? I said, "Thanks anyway." I bolted downstairs to lock all my doors, and windows. I went back upstairs to watch the neighbor's house; I sure wasn't going outside tonight. I knew the police might not send anyone out, so I loaded my handgun, and sat in my chair to wait for the creature to return.

The neighbors were not even home, or at least their car was not in the driveway tonight. I called them but there was no answer. It was going on three in the morning, and then there it was again, the creature from the snow was back, this time it just smashed through the fence, and picked up another dog. I could see his face was red, and his body covered with white hair, large feet, and sharp claws. The legendary lost creature from the Himalayas, was here in Kankakee, but how? The creature again looked up at my window, and screamed into the night. My wife slept right through it all.

The creature began to move towards my house, I ran downstairs, but the creature was at my door, screaming, and pounding to get inside. I was terrified; wondering what was going to happen to me when it got inside. Then it was quiet for a minute, I went to a nearby window, moved the curtain to take a peek. There it was! I was face to face with the snow creature, my eyes were looking directly into his cold blue eyes, and the only thing between him, and I, was the frozen window. The creature let out a loud roar, and then ran off into the blistery night. He could have reached through the glass, and pull me outside, but he didn't, why?

I went back upstairs to look outside once again. The police finally showed up, I saw them walk over to the busted neighbors fence. They found the mutilated bodies of the neighbor's dogs. One of the officers shined the light at the large footprints, and then I saw the light shine up at my face. Both of the officers obviously wondered if I saw anything. One of the officers went through the broken fence that led to the neighbor's back yard; the other one followed the tracks, into the night. I could see the squad car door was left open, and the lights were still flashing. I waited because I knew sooner or later they would be knocking on my front door, looking for answers. An hour went by and it was almost daylight, how strange I thought, that the police never returned to their vehicle.

I saw yet another squad car pull up, then another two police cars behind that one. The area was filled with police; it appeared that a search was underway. Several officers looked up at my candlelit window. Then I heard it, a knock on my front door. I opened the door, and as I did the huge claw mark scratched on my front door, told the whole story. "What happened here last night?" the officer said. "I don't know" I replied, I just woke up! Looks like someone vandalized my door too can you look into it? The officer seemed puzzled by the condition of the door, as he walked away scratching his head. "We'll be in touch, lock your doors" replied the officer.

The next day the headline in the local newspaper read, "Coyotes responsible for attack on local dogs." The two officers were still missing; the police had K-9 units followed the tracks in the snow all day. The interesting part is the second page of the newspaper, many stories of vandalism in the neighborhood, and strange sightings of a snow monster. One story had a photograph of the creature's footprint in the snow. It's late at night, and I am here in my easy chair, with my cat on my lap, a warm blanket, and a cup of hot chocolate staring out of my window at the snow beginning to fall. I wonder what tonight will bring?

The strange creature that came out of the snow, or wherever it came from, may be seen tonight.

The weather is calling for the same below zero weather with lots of snow, perfect weather for a snow creature. I'm glad I do not have any dogs, so he will not come here tonight, and if he does I've had steel doors installed in the front, and back of my house, with bars on the windows. I don't care if no one believes me, although I have told no one, there really is a snow creature in Kankakee. So beware the night, for if you have to travel in the blizzard tonight, you may bump into a hungry snow creature on a rampage looking for a warm meal. As for me, I will just sit in my easy chair, and watch the blizzard to come through my window. As for the barking dogs in the neighborhood, I'll wait for the silence to come, that will be the clue that my cold visitor from a far off place is back for a snack, Stay home tonight!

This is not the end.

Only the beginning of book 4

Soon to hit bookstores, in your area.

Get ready to join Sinister Sam for another walk in the cemeteries, of Kankakee County.